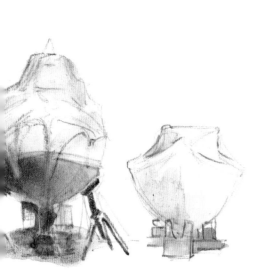

Abrams Books for Young Readers
New York

Sal loved the water.
He liked to imagine it moving under his feet.

He thought about it at
his mom's house,

and at his dad's.

He wanted to be
out there, alone,

just him and the waves.

Sal needed a boat. But he was a kid with
no job, so he couldn't buy one.

He didn't want just any old
regular boat anyway,

so he had to
build it himself.

He started the same way he started all his projects—
by pulling everything out of his mom's garage.

Then he collected whatever Mr. Shipman wouldn't use,

and of course, he checked the Dooly Box at Rose's Marina,
which was always an absolute gold mine.

It wasn't long before everyone started asking about it.

They had tips . . .

and advice for what Sal should do.

He found a place to set up where he
wouldn't be bothered.
(Except maybe by his brother.)

And then Sal got to work.

Measuring

leveling

and snapping chalk lines.

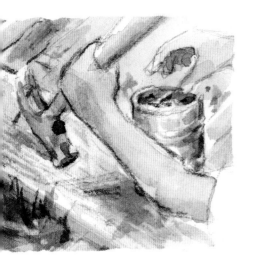

He pulled nails   bent metal   poured paint

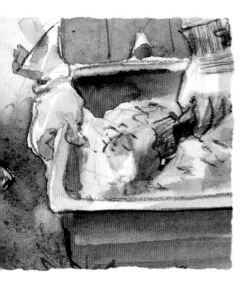

mixed mud   hammered boards   twisted clamps

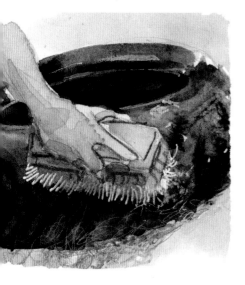

scrubbed rubber   spackled cracks   and napped.

The more Sal worked, the better his ideas got,
and the bigger his plan became.

Sal da Vinci
over here.

snacklace

Foot
cooler

Questions
Complaints
talk
here↑

Soon everyone had their own ideas
of how things should go.

But Sal knew what
he was making.

So they left him alone.

Finally, Sal could make some serious progress.

And after many, many days . . .

. . . his boat was really coming together.

All around town, they were getting it wrong,

So you're building a house?
No! It's a boat.

and misunderstanding,

For your little house.

It's a boat!
But fine, I'll take it.

and maybe making fun of him? He wasn't sure.

For the boat!

But Sal wasn't going to get worked up about it.

What, have they never seen a boat before?
WHAT DO THEY KNOW!
zero imagination in this town.
They don't think I can do it.
I'll show them.
I can do it on my own.
They don't even care what I do anyway.

He didn't want help from anyone.
Not from his mom, or his dad,
and especially not from his brother.

He could finish it himself.

He organized his supplies

swept his deck

arranged his lucky charms

scrubbed the freeboard

polished the equipment

and didn't sleep a wink.

And then Sal's boat was done.

Launch it?

They watched Sal dig,   rig pullies,

and tie ropes.

But nothing worked.

Sal knew it wasn't
their fault.

Suddenly, his boat didn't
seem like a boat at all.

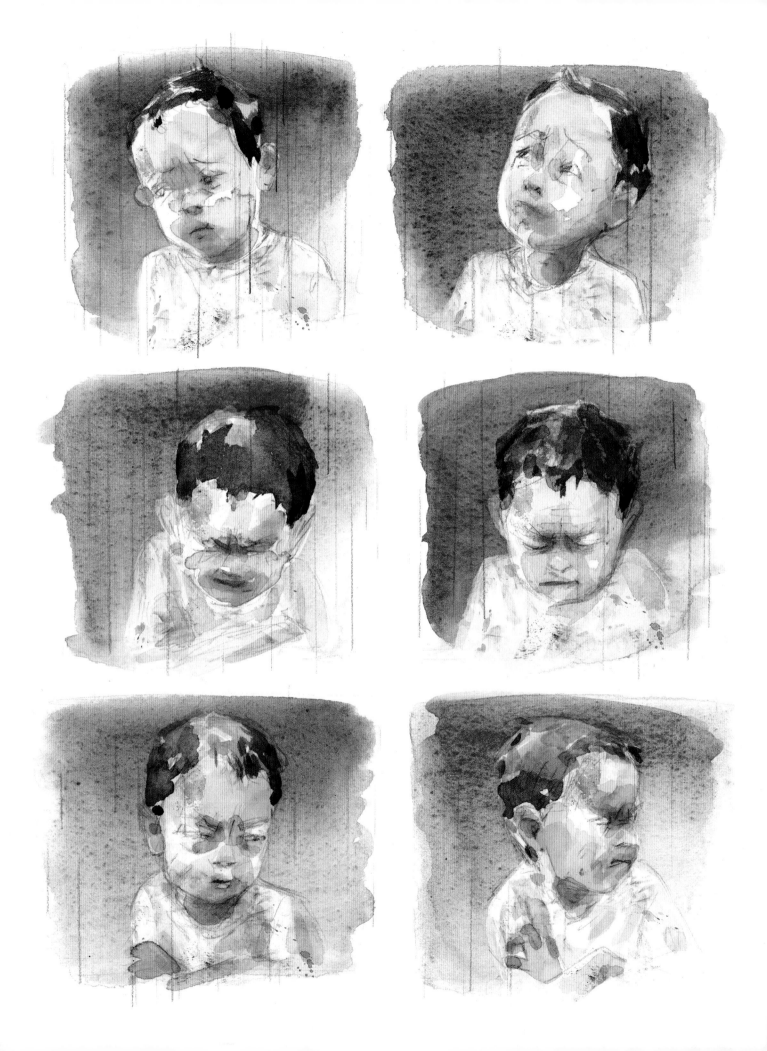

But right before Sal smashed
every dumb shingle and window,
he heard,

WAIT!

Don't touch
that boat!

Everyone showed up to work.

Nobody talked much (except for his brother, who read a poem).

Fair winds and following Seas!

And pretty soon, Sal's boat was ready for a proper launch.

Finally, Sal had his boat.
It was just him
and the waves moving under his feet.

Sal loved the water.
And the best part was . . .

. . . so did everyone else he knew.

A lot of amazing people helped me
make this book. Thank you.

For Milo and Niko

The illustrations in this book were created with
pencils and watercolor.

Cataloging-in-Publication Data has been applied for and may
be obtained from the Library of Congress.

ISBN 978-1-4197-5750-1

Text and illustrations © 2022 Thyra Heder
Book design by Pamela Notarantonio

Printed and bound in China
10 9 8 7 6 5 4 3 2 1

Abrams Books for Young Readers are available at special discounts when
purchased in quantity for premiums and promotions as well as fundraising
or educational use. Special editions can also be created to specification.
For details, contact specialsales@abramsbooks.com or the address below.

Abrams® is a registered trademark of Harry N. Abrams, Inc.

MIX
Paper from
responsible sources
FSC® C144853
www.fsc.org

ABRAMS The Art of Books
195 Broadway, New York, NY 10007
abramsbooks.com